Get to know the girls of

Go Girl! #1: Dancing Queen

Go Girl! #2: Sleepover!

Go Girl! #3: Sister Spirit

Go Girl! #4: The New Girl

Go Girl! #5: The Worst Gymnast

Go Girl! #6: Lunchtime Rules

Go Girl! #7: The Secret Club

Go Girl! #8: Surf's Up!

Go Girl! #9: Camp Chaos

Go Girl! #10: Back to School

Go Girl! #11: Basketball Blues

Go Girl! #12: Catch Me if You Can

THE NEW GIRL

BY
ROWAN McAULEY

ILLUSTRATED BY
ASH OSWALD

SQUARE
FISH

FEIWEL AND FRIENDS
NEW YORK

SQUARE
FISH

An Imprint of Macmillan
175 Fifth Avenue
New York, NY 10010
mackids.com

Square Fish and the Square Fish logo are trademarks of Macmillan
and are used by Feiwel and Friends under license from Macmillan.

Our books may be purchased in bulk for promotional,
educational, or business use. Please contact your local
bookseller or the Macmillan Corporate and Premium Sales
Department at (800) 221-7945 ext. 5442 or by e-mail at
MacmillanSpecialMarkets@macmillan.com.

Library of Congress Cataloging-in-Publication Data Available

ISBN 978-1-250-09814-6

First published in Australia by E2, an imprint of
Hardie Grant Egmont.
Illustration and design by Ash Oswald.

First U.S. Edition: 2008
Square Fish Reissue Edition: 2016
Square Fish logo designed by Filomena Tuosto

1   3   5   7   9   10   8   6   4   2

AR: 3.7

CHAPTER *ONE

One Wednesday morning in the middle of the year, a new girl arrived at Zoe's school. It was the most exciting thing that Zoe could remember happening for ages.

Ms. Kyle knocked on the door during class. Mr. Mack had to stop halfway through a sentence.

Everyone looked up from their books.

"Don't mind us," said Ms. Kyle. "I'm just

talking to Mr. Mack about the new student."

"Wow! A new student," Zoe whispered to her best friend, Iris.

"I know," said Iris. "And what perfect timing. Mr. Mack was speaking way too fast for me to keep up. Quick—while he's still talking to Ms. Kyle—are there two g's in *exaggerated*?"

"Shh," said Zoe. "I'm trying to listen."

But all around her the quiet whispers of the other kids were growing into loud mumblings. She couldn't hear what Ms. Kyle was saying at all.

"Settle down," said Mr. Mack, as Ms. Kyle left. "All right, you all heard that we're getting a new member of our class. Her name is

Isabelle Sinclair, and she will be joining us as soon as she's finished picking up her books and uniform at the office. I know you'll all do your best to make her feel welcome."

Definitely, thought Zoe. *Iris and I will be her best friends.*

"Ok, then," said Mr. Mack. "Let's get back to our vocabulary."

Of course, it was impossible for Zoe to concentrate on her schoolwork. Any minute now, Isabelle could walk through the door. . . .

Zoe wondered what Isabelle would be like. Would she be musical like Iris, funny like Ching Ching, brainy like Chloe, or shy like Olivia?

When Zoe had finished her vocabulary she started drawing little cartoons in the margins of her exercise book. She doodled all the different ways she thought Isabelle might look. Would she be tall or short? Would she have long hair, or—

long hair

short hair

curly hair

"Zoe!" Iris nudged her sharply in the ribs.

Zoe looked up and saw Mr. Mack looking at her pointedly.

"Nice of you to rejoin us, Zoe," he said, dryly.

Zoe quickly sat up straight and covered her drawings with her hand.

"Sorry, Mr. Mack," she said.

Mr. Mack was just about to say something else when there was a knock at the door. It was Ms. Kyle again, followed by a girl in a new school sweater.

Isabelle!

CHAPTER TWO

Isabelle Sinclair stood at the front of the classroom, looking coolly at her new class-mates.

I'd be terrified if that were me, thought Zoe. *I'd be shivering all over.*

But Isabelle looked totally relaxed, even bored.

Ms. Kyle left the room and Mr. Mack turned to Isabelle.

"Well, Isabelle," he said, cheerily. "Welcome to our class. Would you like to tell us a little bit about yourself?"

Oh, no, Mr. Mack! thought Zoe, dismayed. *Don't do that to her!*

Zoe couldn't imagine anything worse on the first day at a new school. She wouldn't have known what to say, and she would have blushed and stammered. But Isabelle spoke confidently.

"My family just moved here because my dad got a transfer at work. He's a lawyer and my mom's a piano teacher. I don't have any brothers or sisters, but I have a weiner dog named Banger who sleeps on my bed."

"Thank you, Isabelle. It's good to have you here," said Mr. Mack. "Why don't you sit at that desk today, and we'll find you a permanent place tomorrow?"

He pointed to Lily's desk.

She was out sick.

The bell rang loudly for lunch, and before Mr. Mack could say another word, everyone had leapt to their feet.

"All right," he called out. "Off you go! Just remember to give Isabelle room to breathe, and time to eat her lunch, while you're busy mobbing her with questions."

Mr. Mack was right—the class *did* mob Isabelle. Everyone wanted to talk to her, be spoken to by her, find out more about her, and tell her about themselves.

"See that mulberry tree over there?" asked Oscar. "That's where Dylan and I climbed out over the school fence."

"We got in the worst trouble," said Dylan, grinning. "They made up a whole new school rule just for us. Now no one is allowed to climb trees."

"And the back of that building is the music room," said Iris, pointing. "We have guitars, a piano, a drum set, and flutes, and everything."

"And next to the music room is the

computer room," said Ching Ching. "We have computer class on Fridays with Mr. Campbell. He's a really good teacher."

Olivia giggled. "You would say that!" she said to Ching Ching. "You've got the biggest crush on him!"

"I so do *not*," said Ching Ching.

"You so do *so*," said Olivia, laughing. "You lo-oo-ove him!"

Zoe was frustrated—she didn't want to hear all this stuff! She wanted to hear about Isabelle. She glanced over and saw Isabelle looking quiet and serious. Zoe realized she hadn't seen Isabelle smile once since she arrived.

By the time lunch was over and they

went back to class, Zoe had only learned
two new things about Isabelle—she used
to have a white Persian cat named Mash,
and her favorite subject was math.

"Hey, I've got an idea!" Zoe whispered
to Iris as they sat down and got their books

out for science. "I'm going to ask my mom if I can have Isabelle over after school. You can come, too, and that way we'll have her all to ourselves."

Iris beamed. "Ask your mom tonight, and then call me. Then I can ask my mom right away and we can invite Isabelle tomorrow."

"Perfect!" smiled Zoe.

It would have been perfect, too, but Zoe never got her chance to invite Isabelle.

CHAPTER THREE

Her troubles began on the way home from school. Most of the kids caught the school bus from the main gates, but the bus didn't go past Zoe's house. Instead, she walked through the playground to where her little brother, Max, was in kindergarten.

Usually Max was annoyingly bouncy, as if he hadn't seen Zoe in a year. But today he slumped against the railings of the school fence as they waited for their mom. It was a warm afternoon and he had his sweater on, but he was still shivering.

"Can I borrow your sweater, Zoe?" he asked, sounding miserable.

Zoe was searching in her bag when her mom drove up.

"Hurry up, Zoe," her mom called out the window. "Can you help Max with his bag? It looks too heavy for him today."

Zoe dumped both bags into the car and jumped in behind them. Max dragged his feet over to the car, looking more tired and sad than ever.

"Max!" said her mom. "Your teeth are

chattering! Zoe, what's wrong with your brother?"

Zoe sighed and shrugged.

Sometimes it was a pain being the big sister. She wanted to talk to her mom about Isabelle, and whether she could have her and Iris over, but now all her mom's attention was on Max.

🐞

By dinnertime, Max's chill had turned into a fever. By breakfast the next morning, he was covered in spots.

"Chicken pox!" said her mom. "How are you feeling, Zoe? Any spots?"

"I'm fine," said Zoe, impatiently. "I just want to get to school."

Her mom didn't seem to notice that Zoe was in a hurry. "Go and get dressed then," she said calmly. "I'm going to have to make a few calls before we go anywhere."

Zoe dressed as quickly as she could while her mom was on the phone. She was just sliding her favorite ladybug hairclip into place when her mom came in.

"Bad news, Zoe," she said. "I called Dr. Ho to get a doctor's note for my work, so I can take time off to look after Max—"

Zoe nodded.

"And Dr. Ho says you'll have to stay home, too."

"What?" gasped Zoe. "But I'm not even sick! Please, Mom, I have to be there today. Can't I—"

"No," said her mom, firmly. "You haven't had chicken pox yet, so there's about a 90-percent chance you've got it now. Dr. Ho says the spots could appear any day."

But I don't have any spots! LOOK!

"But couldn't I go until I get sick?" asked Zoe.

"I'm sorry, Zoe. Even though you don't feel sick yet, you could still pass it on to others. You can't go to school. And no visitors, either. It's just you, Dad, me, and Max."

CHAPTER FOUR

Zoe felt like crying. It was so unfair. She was always missing out. By the time she went back to school, everyone would know Isabelle except for her.

That afternoon, the phone rang while Max and Zoe were on the sofa watching TV.

"Zoe," called her mom. "It's Iris for you."

Zoe got up slowly. She was surprised to find she was feeling dizzy and cold.

"Hi, Iris," she said.

"Zoe, you didn't call me last night. And then I was worried when you didn't come to school today."

"Didn't Mr. Mack tell you? Max has chicken pox, and I probably have it, too, so we have to stay home."

"For how long?"

"At least a week."

"A week!" cried Iris. "That's forever."

"Or longer," said Zoe. "We can't leave the house until our spots scab over."

"Scab over? Gross! How many spots do you have?"

"None yet," said Zoe, feeling even worse. "Anyway, tell me. How was school?

Did you hang out with Isabelle?"

"Yeah, you'll never guess—Mr. Mack put her at our table. She's sitting next to me!"

"Really? What's she like?"

"Oh, she's so funny! You won't believe what she did! When Mr. Campbell came in for computers, Isabelle made this kissing noise, and Ching Ching turned bright red in front of everyone!"

"Ha ha," laughed Zoe, sadly. She wished she could have been there.

"And then," Iris went on, "at lunch, Isabelle dared Dylan to sneak out the gates and run to the corner and back."

"No way!" said Zoe.

"Yep. And Dylan said he wouldn't, because he and Oscar got in so much trouble last time they snuck out. So Isabelle went herself! And she didn't run, either. She just walked out, like it was no big deal."

"Wow," said Zoe, impressed. "So Isabelle's pretty cool, then?"

"The coolest."

"Oh," said Zoe, in a small voice. "Good."

CHAPTER FIVE

It took more than a week for Zoe to get over the chicken pox. The spots were terrible—itchy and sore, and she even had some up her nose! At last they dried up, though, and she could go back to school.

She had been away for so long, Zoe felt like *she* was the new girl. Her face was covered in little scabs and she didn't know what had been going on while she was away. Maybe no one was into hopscotch anymore, and she'd look like a big nerd for wanting to play.

When she arrived at school she saw Iris standing around chatting with Isabelle. Isabelle had her notebook out and they were reading through something together.

"Hi," she called out, shifting her backpack.

For a tiny fraction of a second, before saying hello, Iris looked at Isabelle, as if she were checking what she should do. It happened so fast, Zoe almost didn't see it.

Almost.

"Hi, Zoe," Iris said, carefully.

"Yeah, hi," said Isabelle, looking at her watch.

Iris looked uncomfortable.

Finally she said, "Um, we're just finishing this math problem before the bell rings. I'll talk to you later, OK?"

Zoe didn't know what to do. She stood there, feeling every single scab on her face. She was sure that everyone else in the playground was staring at her. She was so embarrassed. She wished she could laugh and pretend it didn't matter, but it did.

It *hurt*.

Zoe went to the bathroom and looked at her face in the mirror. *It must be the chicken pox*, she thought. Probably nobody wanted to play with a spotty, scabby girl.

She heard voices behind her, and Ching

Ching and Holly came in. Quickly, Zoe started washing her hands, as though she had just been to the bathroom.

"Hi, Zoe," said Ching Ching. "I didn't know you were back today."

"Um, hi," said Zoe, wondering if Ching Ching and Holly could tell how upset she was. She wondered if they had seen what happened on the playground.

"Hey, you have to talk to Isabelle," said Holly. "She's organized a jump rope contest at lunchtime, with real scores and play-offs and a championship and everything. You have to enter!"

"Oh," said Zoe. "I don't have a jump rope."

"No problem," said Ching Ching. "You can borrow mine."

"The bell!" said Holly. "We'd better hurry. Mr. Mack went *mental* when we were late for class yesterday."

CHAPTER SIX

Zoe was in no hurry. She had been so desperate to come back to school, but now that she was here, she wished she were home again.

"Hey, Zoe," said Mr. Mack, standing by the door of the classroom. "How was the chicken pox? Itchy, I bet."

"Yes, Mr. Mack," said Zoe.

"Well, you're back just in time," he said.

"We're starting a new project today, and it should be really interesting."

"OK," she said, not really listening.

They walked into the classroom, and Zoe looked at the desk where she normally sat. Iris and Isabelle were already there, getting their pens and pencils out and giggling about something.

Zoe took a deep breath and went to sit

with them. She didn't say anything—she felt too shy.

This is crazy, she thought. *How can I be feeling shy in front of my own best friend?*

She hoped that Iris would say something so that everything could go back to normal, but Iris just gave her a little smile when Isabelle wasn't looking.

"Good morning, all," said Mr. Mack. "Did anyone *not* do last night's homework?"

Mr. Mack walked around the room, collecting assignments.

"It's OK, Zoe," he said as he took Iris and Isabelle's work. "I know you haven't done this one. So," he said to the rest of the class, "I'm going to start marking these at my desk while you do the math problems I've written out on these worksheets."

Everyone groaned.

"What?" asked Mr. Mack, pretending to be surprised. "What's this I hear? Is my class telling me they want *more* work-sheets? Are they complaining I haven't given them *enough* math problems? OK, then. Get on with what I've given you. And no group discussion. That means you, Oscar Morgan. If you have a question, raise your hand. Otherwise I want *silence*."

Usually Zoe hated starting off with silent work, but today she was glad to put her head down and not have to talk to anyone. She didn't want to even look at

Iris or Isabelle until they said something nice to her. She hoped she wouldn't have to wait long.

When the bell rang for recess, most of the girls gathered around Isabelle.

"Who's in the first round today?" asked Chloe.

Isabelle pulled out her notebook and opened it to a page of complicated looking tables.

"Let's see," she said. "We're up to round two. Chloe, you'll be jumping against Ching Ching and Holly. And then Iris,

Olivia, and Lily will be in round three at lunchtime."

Zoe hadn't said anything to Isabelle yet. All morning, she had kept her eyes on her work and tried not to notice when Iris and Isabelle whispered to one another. Now, without knowing how she managed to be so brave, she spoke up.

"Can I be in the competition, too?" Zoe asked.

Isabelle looked at her.

"No," she said. "We had the qualifying rounds while you were away. Now that we've already begun, it wouldn't really be fair to let you enter in round four or five."

"But I had the chicken pox!" said Zoe.

She couldn't believe her ears.

"Well, we have to be fair," said Isabelle. "It's not a real contest unless you stick to the rules."

"I see," said Zoe, in a tiny voice.

"Hey, but Zoe could help us judge," Iris said to Isabelle. "Couldn't she?"

Isabelle thought for a minute and then shook her head.

"I'm *so* sorry," she said, without sounding sorry at all. "But only girls who are part of the competition are allowed to judge."

Zoe felt small and unwanted.

How embarrassing. And in front of all the other girls! Now everyone knew that she had been left out.

CHAPTER
SEVEN

Zoe wanted to cry, or better still, to disappear forever. But the bell had rung and Mr. Mack was waiting in the hallway to lock the classroom door behind them.

Zoe got her snack out of her bag and somehow managed to walk out to the playground without bursting into tears. She saw Iris by herself, peeling an orange beside the trash can.

Now's my chance, she thought. *I'll go and ask Iris if I've done something wrong.*

She hurried over and said in a quiet, uncertain voice, "Hi, Iris."

"Oh, Zoe," said Iris, smiling. "How are you? I've been wanting to talk to you all day."

"Have you?" said Zoe, feeling relieved. "I thought nobody liked me anymore."

"Oh, no," said Iris. "That's not true."

"What's not true?"

Iris and Zoe spun around to see Isabelle standing there.

"Nothing," said Zoe. "I was just talking to Iris."

"Well, Iris can't stand around talking," said Isabelle in a bossy voice. "She needs to come with me and help judge round two of the contest."

"But Zoe can come and watch, can't she?" asked Iris.

Isabelle looked at Zoe thoughtfully.

"I don't want to sound mean or anything," she said. "But your scabs are kind of icky. Maybe you could go and play with someone else instead."

Oh ... I wish my spots would go away!

Zoe was so shocked she couldn't think of a single thing to say. *Nobody* had ever said anything so cruel to her in her life.

She was still standing there when Isabelle turned and began to walk away.

"Come on, Iris," said Isabelle. "We won't get through round two if we don't hurry up. We can't keep wasting time like this."

Iris looked as shocked as Zoe felt. Iris was about to say something when Isabelle called out loudly, "Iris!"

Iris gave Zoe a sad, guilty look, and turned to follow Isabelle.

This must be a nightmare, thought Zoe. *This can't be real. This is my school. These are my friends. Why am I the one being left out?*

She saw the other girls lined up for the competition. Some of them had jump ropes, others had paper for writing down the scores. They looked so far away, like they were all part of another world.

I'm all alone now!

Zoe knew that she couldn't go over now—she didn't even know if she wanted to anymore. And Isabelle had made it quite clear that she wasn't welcome.

Zoe didn't know what to do, but she didn't want to stand there on her own.

She knew the boys would let her play with them if she asked. They were running around with a football, yelling and cheering. It would take a lot of energy to join in their game, though, and Zoe didn't have any energy now. It felt like Isabelle's nasty comments had drained all the life out of her.

"Hello there, Zoe," said Mrs. Delano, walking by on playground duty. "First day back since the chicken pox, isn't it?"

Zoe nodded.

"You still look a little pale, actually. Do you feel all right, dear?"

No, I don't, thought Zoe. *I feel terrible!*

She didn't say anything, though. She thought she might cry if she tried to speak. Instead, she shook her head.

"Why don't I take you to the nurse's office?" said Mrs. Delano, kindly. "You can rest until you feel better."

CHAPTER EIGHT

Normally, Zoe thought the nurse's office was boring. It was the smallest, ugliest room in the school. There were no pictures to look at, no books to read, and nothing to do but lie there.

On any other day, Zoe would have done anything to get out of there, but right now it felt safe and cozy.

Every now and then, Ms. Kyle would

come in and ask, "Are you feeling any better? Shall I call your mom?"

Each time, Zoe shook her head. She *wasn't* feeling better, but she couldn't call her mom, either. She knew her mom couldn't take any more time off work.

Zoe was stuck at school. Eventually, the bell rang. She gave a huge sigh and went back to class.

It seemed like a miracle to Zoe that she made it through the whole day without crying. She concentrated as hard as she could on her work, hoping it would block out all her unhappy thoughts, and some-how she survived until the bell rang.

By the time she got home and changed

out of her clothes, she was feeling angry
as well as sad. And it wasn't Isabelle she
was most angry at. It was Iris!

She decided to call her.

Iris answered the phone right away.

"Hello? This is Iris."

"Hello, Iris," said Zoe.

"Zoe! Hi—"

Zoe interrupted her. She didn't want to hear what Iris was going to say. She just wanted to know one thing.

"Why didn't you stick up for me at school? You're supposed to be my best friend, but you didn't even talk to me!"

There was a silence, and then Iris said, "I'm sorry, Zoe. I am still your friend, but now I'm Isabelle's friend, too."

"What's that supposed to mean?"

"When you were away," said Iris, "I had no one to play with. And Isabelle had no one either, so we ended up playing together."

"Right," said Zoe. "So?"

"Well, now you're back, and you have

lots of other friends you can play with. Lots of people know you, but Isabelle has only me. Isabelle really needs me, Zoe. More than you do."

"What are you talking about?" asked Zoe. "It doesn't make sense. Why can't you play with me and Isabelle at the same time?"

"You wouldn't understand," said Iris. "It's really hard for Isabelle, being new. She says she needs me all to herself until she settles in."

So that's it, thought Zoe, when she hung up the phone. *Now Isabelle is Iris's best friend, and there's no room for me.*

CHAPTER NINE

The next day at school, Zoe watched Iris and Isabelle stand together while everyone crowded around them to talk about the jump rope contest. Iris looked happy about being so popular and important. Isabelle chewed the end of her hair and ticked things off in her notebook.

Nobody noticed Zoe standing by herself, watching. They were all too excited about the contest. Everyone wanted to be in it, and that meant there was no one left over for Zoe to hang out with. Even Lily, who hated sports, had brought her own jump rope to school.

All recess and all lunch, and anytime they could squeeze in before school or before the bus came to take them home, all anyone wanted to do was jump rope. And in class, when people passed notes or whispered to one another, it was jump rope they were talking about.

It was the biggest craze Zoe had ever seen, and she was completely left out of it.

And worse than all that, her best friend was now best friends with the meanest, nastiest girl in the whole school.

All in all, it was the most horrible week at school Zoe could remember.

On Tuesday, Zoe visited Max in the kindergarten playground.

There is nothing to do at lunchtime now!

On Wednesday, she went back to the nurse's office at recess and lunch, and pretended to have a headache.

On Thursday, she went to the library at

recess. At lunch, though, the library was closed because the librarian had to go to the dentist. So Zoe went back to the nurse.

I can't believe how things have turned out, she thought, as she lay back on the cold bed. *How did I end up being so unpopular? Why does everyone like Isabelle better than me?*

When the bell rang for class, Zoe panicked.

I'm not ready to see Isabelle again, she thought.

Then she tried to encourage herself. *Come on, Zoe. It's art class this afternoon— your favorite.*

She straggled into class behind everyone else and saw that Mr. Mack had put out jars of paint and paintbrushes.

"Today," said Mr. Mack, "we won't be painting people or other ordinary things. Instead, I want you to paint *feelings*."

"What do you mean?" said Dylan. "Like painting a sad face or a happy face?"

"No. I mean, if you felt really happy, for example, what color would that be? Or what shape might you paint to show anger? Or excitement?"

There was some mumbling among the class, but Zoe knew exactly what Mr. Mack meant. And she knew exactly what she was going to paint.

Just before the bell rang, Mr. Mack asked them to finish their paintings and hang them up to dry. As each kid pegged up their work, Mr. Mack talked to them about what they had painted.

"Wonderful," he said to Holly. "Everyone, look at how Holly has used pink circles, one inside the other, to show love. It's like lots of hugs at once. Oh, and that's terrific, Oscar. Jagged black and red lightning bolts. Anger, right?"

Zoe brought her painting up.

"Zoe, this is beautiful. All different shades of blue and purple, like deep water or a stormy sky. What is it? Sadness?"

"No," said Zoe, very, very quietly, so no one would hear her. "It's loneliness."

Mr. Mack was silent for a moment, and then he said, "Thank you, Zoe. It's marvelous. I can see just what you feel."

CHAPTER TEN

These days, Zoe was glad she didn't ride the bus with the rest of her class. It suited her perfectly to sit in the back of the car and stare out the window as they drove home.

That afternoon, Max told their mom a long story about what he did on the monkey bars at lunch. It lasted the whole trip, and Zoe didn't have to say one word.

When they got home, Zoe dragged her backpack out of the car and shuffled her way up the steps of the house.

"You OK, Zoe?" said her mom. "You're extra quiet this afternoon."

Zoe shrugged.

"She's in a bad mood," said Max. "She wouldn't talk to me while we were waiting for you. She's always in a bad mood. A moo-oo-oo-ood! A moo-oo-oo—OW!"

"Zoe!" said her mom. "Don't you *dare* hit your brother! What kind of behavior is that? Say sorry immediately."

Without warning, all of the bad feelings of the week suddenly washed over Zoe. She was sick and tired of being left out and feeling unloved and having people be mean to her.

"I'm not sorry!" she yelled. "He should be sorry, not me! I'm *not* in a bad mood!"

"Zoe, you go to your room right now before I give you something to really be sorry for!"

"Yeah, Zoe," said Max, rubbing his arm. "You're a meanie."

"I hate you!" Zoe screamed at him.

"Zoe!" shouted her mom. "Go now!"

Zoe burst into tears and ran to her room. She lay down on her bed and cried and cried. She had stopped herself from crying so many times at school, it was a relief to be able to cry out loud at last.

After a while, the tears slowed down, and she started to think about school.

How was she possibly going to survive another day? She couldn't, it was as simple as that. She would just have to tell her mom she wasn't going back.

CHAPTER ELEVEN

That evening, Zoe had dinner in her room. She refused to say sorry to Max for hitting him, and her mom said she had to stay in her room until she did. Zoe didn't care. She was better off on her own. She was even starting to get used to it. She was on her own all day at school, and then on her own at home. One day she'd vanish for good, and nobody would even notice.

"Zoe?"

It was her dad, home from work and tapping on her door. Zoe sat up on her bed.

"Mom said you had a fight with Max this afternoon."

Zoe sighed. *Here we go*, she thought.

Her dad sat on the end of her bed.

"This isn't like you, Zoe," he said. "You don't usually hit or shout, and you don't usually say you're not sorry. Mom says there's some trouble at school."

Zoe nodded.

"Is it Iris?" asked her dad.

"Sort of. Iris didn't start it, but she didn't stick up for me, either, so I'm mad at her, too."

"Start what? What's been happening?"

"There's a new girl at school called Isabelle. She's horrible, and she hates me, and now I hate her."

"You hate her?"

"Yes, I do," said Zoe. "She's a bully. I

wish I could pay her back for how mean she's been to me."

Zoe went on to tell him everything that had happened at school.

"Yes, I see," said her dad. "You must be really angry with Iris *and* Isabelle."

"I am," said Zoe.

"Isabelle really hurt your feelings."

"Yes," said Zoe. "Exactly."

Phew, she thought. *At least Dad understands.*

"Hmm," said her dad.

"What do you think I should do?" asked Zoe. "How can I make her sorry for what she's done to me?"

"That's a good question. There are two ways you can handle this Isabelle," said her dad. "The first way is to spend lots of time brooding about how much you hate her and thinking up ways to hurt her feelings the way she has hurt yours."

"Yes, yes," said Zoe, eagerly. "I could make her feel stupid in front of everyone."

"Yes, you could," said her dad. "But then, on the other hand, that might just make her angry. And if you *do* get her back and make her feel bad—well, aren't you being just as big a bully as she is?"

"No!" said Zoe. "How am I a bully if she started it in the first place? Doesn't it serve her right?"

"Maybe," said her dad. "But I'm not really thinking about what Isabelle deserves. I'm thinking about you, and I don't think you're the sort of girl who enjoys being cruel."

Zoe wasn't sure her dad was right. She had been imagining some great ways of making Isabelle cry in front of the whole school. It had been the only fun thing she'd done all week.

"I like the first idea," she said. "But tell me anyway—what's the other way?"

CHAPTER TWELVE

"The second way," said her dad, "is to stand tall. You don't stoop to her level, and you don't fight back. You stand tall and act with pride, because in the long run, a bully will trip herself up. The other kids will see soon enough who is the better friend."

"That's it?" said Zoe, unimpressed. "That's my secret plan? To be *nice*? I just hang around waiting for Isabelle to get bored of being mean?"

"Yep," said her dad. "It won't be easy, though."

"No kidding" said Zoe. "I don't think it will work at all."

"Oh, it will work. Don't worry about that. You might not think so, but being kind and treating people with respect is very powerful."

Zoe looked at her dad. He looked completely serious. He wasn't joking.

"I don't think I can do it, Dad," she said, at last. "I'm so angry with her, I don't want to be nice."

"I know," said her dad, kissing her. "But you're a terrific kid, Zoe. You'll do the right thing. Now come outside, say sorry to your brother, and you can have some dessert."

The next day was Friday, and Zoe tried hard to remember what her dad had said. She tried to think calm, kind thoughts. She imagined Isabelle's mean comments just pinging off her, as if she were bullet-proof.

Sticks and stones, she thought. *Words can never hurt me.*

But when she saw Isabelle standing in a group with Iris, her heart skipped a beat and she felt afraid.

Nobody will be on my side, she thought. *They all want to be Isabelle's friend. What's the point of standing tall if you still end up with no one to play with?*

Oh ... what's the point of standing tall?

She bit her lip and walked toward them. *Oh, well*, she thought. *Here goes nothing....*

"Hi, Iris," she said. "Hi, Isabelle."

"Hi, Zoe," said Iris, smiling.

"Iris, we have to organize the jump rope

play-offs at recess," said Isabelle, as if she hadn't heard Zoe speak.

"How is the contest going?" asked Zoe, determined to be friendly.

"Look, Zoe," said Isabelle. "Iris and I are very busy. Please don't interrupt our conversation again."

Zoe gasped. How could she keep on being nice to such a mean girl? Her dad wanted her to stand tall, but Zoe felt as though she were shrinking inside.

CHAPTER THIRTEEN

That lunchtime, some of the girls who had dropped out of Isabelle's contest got bored of sitting around watching other people jump rope. For the first time in ages, there were other girls to play with and other games to play. Zoe played handball with Chloe, Holly, Sophie, Ching Ching, and Olivia.

Zoe was glad she had people to play

Wow!
I have some
friends again!

with, and glad that Isabelle couldn't stop everyone from being friends with her. But she still missed Iris. Even though she was mad at Iris for liking Isabelle more than her, Zoe still wanted to be friends with her. It just wasn't the same playing with others.

As she was thinking about this and eating her lunch, Sophie asked her, "How come you don't play with Iris anymore? Did you have a fight?"

Zoe didn't know what to say. Her dad wanted her to stand tall, but it would be so easy right now to tell Sophie how horrible she thought Isabelle was and how dumb she thought Iris was being. She hadn't yet decided what to say when Sophie nodded and said, "It's that Isabelle, isn't it? You know, I think she's a bully."

Just then, Ching Ching howled in frustration. She had missed an easy shot in handball. She left the square and let Olivia take her place, and sat down next to Zoe.

"Are you talking about Isabelle?" Ching Ching asked.

"Yeah," said Sophie.

"She's such bad news," said Ching Ching. "You know, she even told me I should stop being friends with Olivia if I wanted to play with her. Can you believe it?"

"What did you say?" asked Zoe.

"Huh! I told her to get lost. Who cares about jump rope, anyway?"

Dad was right, thought Zoe. *Isabelle is starting to trip up.*

After lunch, in the last hour before the weekend, Mr. Mack said, "Poetry now! I want each of you to spend some time looking at the painting you did yesterday.

Then, when you're ready, we're going to write poems about those feelings."

Zoe looked up at the wall where her painting had been pinned. It was next to Isabelle's. Isabelle had painted a black and grey cloud, and Zoe wondered what it meant. Maybe Isabelle's feeling was hate— maybe she had painted how she felt about Zoe! That was a scary thought, and Zoe quickly went back to her own painting.

After a couple of minutes, she started to write her poem.

"OK," said Mr. Mack. "The bell is about to ring. When you've finished your poems, pack up your things quietly, and please hand in your work on your way out. I'm very interested to see what each of you has written."

Zoe was very interested, too. Although she knew Isabelle would hate her to peek, she glanced over to see what Isabelle had written. It was a long poem with lots of crossing out in tiny, neat writing. It was difficult to read upside down. Zoe could only read the title.

What is Isabelle writing about?

It was called "Homesickness."

Oh! thought Zoe. *Isabelle's homesick? I never would have guessed!*

"What are you looking at?" asked Isabelle. She must have been chewing her hair again, because the end of her ponytail was soggy.

"Nothing," said Zoe, looking away.

"Good. You should mind your own business."

She might be homesick, thought Zoe. *But she's still mean.*

She went out to the locker room to pack her bag for home. She thought she'd gotten everything and was halfway across the playground to meet up with Max and her mom, when she remembered that she had left behind her notebook. She'd have to go back and get it.

She ran back into the locker room, trying to hurry so she didn't keep her mom waiting. She was in such a hurry, she didn't notice at first that she wasn't alone.

There was someone else in the room.

Oh, no! thought Zoe. *Isabelle! Well, I won't say anything to her, and she will hopefully leave me alone, too.*

But then she heard something amazing.

Isabelle was crying.

CHAPTER
FOURTEEN

What should Zoe do? Should she pretend she couldn't hear Isabelle crying? What would she say, anyway?

Then Zoe had an idea. *I could show her what it's like*, she thought. *I could say, "What a crybaby you turned out to be!"*

After a whole week of being picked on, Zoe felt like it would be nice to pay Isabelle back a bit. . . .

But she knew her dad was right.

Although it was fun to imagine, Zoe didn't think she could really say any of the things she was thinking. Zoe didn't like seeing people hurt or upset. To her surprise, that even included Isabelle. She stood awkwardly for a while and then went over to Isabelle's locker.

"Are you OK?" she said.

"Go away!" said Isabelle, sniffing.

It was hard to be scared of her, though, when she sounded so sad. Zoe took a deep breath and stood as tall as she could. She was about to try something brave, and she wasn't sure how it would turn out.

"I'm sorry you're unhappy," she said.

"Is there anything I can do?"

Isabelle looked at her in surprise.

"Why are you being so nice to me?" she asked.

Zoe shrugged.

"I hate it here," Isabelle blurted out. "I miss my old school, and nobody here cares about me."

"What do you mean?" said Zoe, amazed. "Everyone here is your friend." She took another deep breath. "Even I would be, if you let me," she added.

"You! Why would *you* want to be my friend?"

It was hard to come up with a good answer right away. Honestly, Zoe wasn't

100-percent sure she really *did* want to be Isabelle's friend right now. But then she thought about what school had been like before Isabelle came, when everyone got along.

"It's better if we're all friends, don't you think?" she said, at last. "No one should be left out."

Isabelle blinked and sniffed. Then she stuck out her chin and said, "Are you going to tell everyone you saw me cry?"

"Of course not!" said Zoe. "I would never do that."

"Well, OK, then," said Isabelle, smiling very slightly.

Zoe thought it was the first real smile

she had seen on Isabelle's face.

"So," said Zoe. "Friends?"

Isabelle nodded. A tiny nod, but a nod all the same. Zoe was relieved.

"I'll see you on Monday," said Isabelle. "I'd better go. My mom's probably waiting for me."

"Oh, no!" said Zoe, grabbing her notebook. "I forgot! My mom's waiting, too!"

She waved good-bye and started to run back to meet Max and her mom. She just left the locker room and started sprinting for the stairs when she heard Mr. Mack call her name behind her.

Uh-oh, thought Zoe. *Caught running in the hallway.*

But Mr. Mack was not angry with her.

"I heard all that," he said, as Zoe walked back to him. "Your conversation with Isabelle, I mean. The last couple of days have been pretty hard for you, haven't they?"

Zoe shrugged, embarrassed. She didn't think anyone had noticed.

"But still, you were kind to Isabelle just then. You could have left her feeling miserable, but instead you made a new friend. I'm proud of you, Zoe."

Zoe was so pleased, she didn't know what to say. She blushed and then said awkwardly, "Um, thanks. I've got to go. Mom's waiting in the car."

"Off you go, then," said Mr. Mack. "Have

a good weekend!"

Zoe ran through the school as fast as her legs could carry her.

This is still my place, she thought. *I still belong here. And I did it! Wait till I tell Dad. I stood tall!*

CHAPTER FIFTEEN

That evening, Iris called Zoe.

"Um, Zoe? It's Iris."

"Hi, Iris," said Zoe, carefully.

"I just spoke to Isabelle. . . . "

"Yeah?"

"She said you were really nice to her, and she felt bad about how mean she's been to you."

"Oh, right," said Zoe, wondering what

was going on.

"I'm really sorry, too," said Iris. "I got all caught up in being friends with Isabelle and I pretended I didn't notice how horrible she was to you. I was a bad friend, and I don't blame you if you're mad at me."

The funny thing was, even though Zoe had been very angry with Iris, as soon as she said she was sorry, Zoe forgave her entirely. She just wanted to be friends again.

"I really missed you, Zoe."

"I missed you, too," said Zoe.

Next Monday morning, Zoe felt nervous and excited at the same time. What if Isabelle had changed her mind over the weekend and decided to keep on being mean to Zoe?

There was only one way to find out, but Zoe couldn't stand the suspense.

As her mom pulled up outside the school gates, Zoe could see Iris and Isabelle sitting together on a bench, talking. Zoe bit her nails nervously.

"Are you getting out?" asked her mom.

"I guess so," said Zoe.

Oh, well, she thought. *I can always go back to the nurse's office.*

She picked up her bag and got out of

the car. She walked over to the others. Isabelle was chewing her hair, looking like she was waiting for something bad to happen. When she saw Zoe, she gave a little jump and then stood up.

"Hi, Zoe," she said shyly. "Um, I have something for you. I made it with my mom yesterday."

As Isabelle went to her bag, Zoe looked at Iris. Iris smiled, but didn't say anything. Isabelle brought out a plastic lunchbox and handed it to Zoe.

"Here," she said.

Zoe pulled off the lid. Inside was a square cake, about the size of a very fat sandwich. It had thick chocolate icing with

"SORRY, ZOE" spelled out across the top in tiny blue sugar stars.

"It's a mud cake," said Isabelle. "My mom baked it, but I decorated it myself."

"It's great!" said Zoe. "When can we eat it?"

"It's all for you," said Isabelle. "You can eat it whenever you like. You can even keep the lunchbox, if you want—"

"Oh, no," said Zoe. "We should definitely eat it together. And in fact, we should eat it right now!"

"Zoe!" laughed Iris. "We just had breakfast!"

"So?" said Zoe. "This is a special cake. I don't think we should wait around."

Iris and Isabelle didn't need much convincing. Zoe cut the cake into three rectangles, using the ruler from her geometry set as a knife.

Quick as anything, before the bell rang for class, they each took a piece and wolfed it down!

It really was the most delicious cake. Zoe couldn't think of a better way to start a brand-new week. A new beginning with the new girl, making up with Iris, plus the tastiest chocolate mud cake, too.

THE END

Gemma loves gymnastics. But she's just had the worst class EVER, and her coach isn't happy. Is Gemma's life as a gymnast over?

Keep reading for an excerpt!

CHAPTER ❋ ONE

Gemma stood at the start of the runway, ready to run. She pictured a handspring in her mind—*legs together, butt tucked in . . . up and over the vault*. But she didn't run yet. She was waiting for Michael to nod his head.

Michael was Gemma's gymnastics coach. He kicked a safety mat into place, then stood next to the vault, ready to help Gemma over.

Finally, Michael nodded his head.

Gemma wiped her hands on her legs and looked at the vault. Then she ran.

She ran fast, pumping her arms.

As Gemma ran up to the vault, Michael reached in to help her over.

But as Gemma jumped, her foot slipped. Her legs flew apart and her butt stuck out. She did it all wrong. She was just about to crash into the vault when Michael pushed her up and over—*legs apart, butt out, almost over* . . .

Thud!

One of Gemma's legs—out of control —hit Michael in the face. Gemma landed on her back, with her arms and legs out.

It had been a very bad vault.

Gemma lay on her back, surprised that
she had made it over. That had been close.
Was anything hurt? Nothing.

Then Gemma remembered the thud.
She rolled off the mat.

Michael stood in the same spot with
his face in his hands.

"Sorry," Gemma said quietly.

This was bad. Was Michael alright?

"I'm so sorry," Gemma said a bit louder.

Michael lifted his head.

Blood trickled from his nose onto the palm of his hand.

"Are you alright?" Gemma asked, but it felt like a silly question. His nose was bleeding.

Michael looked at Gemma and shook his head. He wiped his nose with a tissue. "Team meeting," he said, and walked away.

The rest of the team was sitting at the start of the runway. The four girls sat in a row with their mouths dropped open and their eyes wide. They looked as if they had just seen a ghost. Either that, or the worst vault ever.

Gemma sat down next to her best friend, Kathy. Kathy had dark curly hair that bounced when she moved, and a broad smile. Gemma thought Kathy was beautiful.

Kathy looked at Gemma as if to say, *We're in for it now.*

Gemma raised her eyebrows back at Kathy. Was she about to be kicked off the team?

Michael was a good coach, the best at the club. But he yelled a lot. Most of the gymnasts were afraid of him. He had hairy eyebrows that made it look like he was always frowning.

"You don't have to like me. But you have to listen to me!" Michael would often yell at the girls.

So kicking him in the face was not very good at all.

"OK, level six," Michael wiped his nose again. "It's time to talk."

The five girls sat in a row. For the next ten minutes, they listened to Michael. He talked, he frowned, he yelled. For the whole ten minutes, the girls didn't move.

Gemma loved gymnastics. Her school friends called her "Gemma the gymnast." But they had no idea how hard Gemma worked at it.

She had worked so hard that she was

now on a real team. Being on a team meant that she had her own routines and entered competitions. Soon, the level six team would go to the state finals.

But being on a team meant more than that. It meant that Michael was Gemma's coach. And Michael was the top coach. Some of the girls on his teams had even made it to the Olympics. So Gemma was delighted to be on Michael's team.

Now Michael talked about working hard—harder than ever before. He talked about what it takes to be the best.

"It's time to get serious," he said.

At the end of his talk, Michael sent the rest of the team to the bars.

OH, NO:
Is my life as
a gymnast over?

Then he looked at Gemma. "Let's go to my office," he said.

Gemma looked at the floor and nodded. She swallowed a big lump in her throat. This was it. Her life as a gymnast was over.

She was about to be kicked off the team.

When one of the boys decides Ant
(short for Samantha) is too slow
to play sports with them, Ant feels
completely left out. Can she come up
with a plan to turn things around?

Keep reading for an excerpt!

CHAPTER ONE

If this lunchtime doesn't end soon, I'm going to explode. It's gone on forever and ever and I'm sick of it. I'm sure the bell should have rung ages ago.

It's been another horrible, endless lunchtime. Just like all the others since everything went wrong and my friends started playing without me.

I can hear them, just over there behind

me, playing soccer. My favorite. My best friend Ellie is shouting our cheer song. That's what we always shouted when we won against the boys.

It's just so unfair! Hearing Ellie makes my eyes sting. I stare into my lunch box, which looks all blurry. The girls I'm sitting with haven't noticed yet—they're busy talking. I really don't want to start crying in front of them, so I blink my eyes hard and try to stop my breath from coming out in little shudders.

"Ellie, you're a cheat!" I hear Red shout from behind me. He always says that when he loses. Red is good at sports but he's not very smart, so if he loses he can't quite figure out what happened. Some kids call him Red the Brain Dead, but I think he's OK, really. Ellie and I have been playing games at lunchtime with Red and his best friend Nick since the beginning of second grade.

Until now, that is.

"She *didn't cheat!*" I hear Lauren shout back. Lauren has taken my place as Ellie's partner. She always wanted to play with us, but our rules needed four players. Five just didn't work. But now I'm not there. . . .

This is so dumb!

How can they play without me? I can't believe they've just replaced me, as if I didn't matter! I was always the one who got us going! I was the one who made up new rules when we needed them! I was the one who always stopped Red and Nick from fighting! And if it hadn't been for me, there wouldn't have been any Grand Final competition and party, because they would *never* have thought of

it! Now, there they are, just playing away like everything is normal.

A huge sob forces its way up my throat. Karen, sitting next to me, looks over. "Are you OK?" she asks. Karen is kind to everyone.

I nod my head, but my breathing has started to come in gasps and everything's gone blurry again.

"It must be awful not playing," she says gently. "You're so good at all those games, even though you're small."